Kerfuffle Bird

For Tom, with all my love—H.D. x

To Louise, with love—G.M. x

OXFORD
UNIVERSITY PRESS

Great Clarendon Street, Oxford OX2 6DP

Oxford University Press is a department of the University of Oxford.
It furthers the University's objective of excellence in research, scholarship,
and education by publishing worldwide. Oxford is a registered trade mark
of Oxford University Press in the UK and in certain other countries

British Library Cataloguing in Publication Data

Data available

ISBN: 978-1-38-205382-2

1 3 5 7 9 10 8 6 4 2

The manufacturing process conforms to the
environmental regulations of the country of origin.

Printed in China

The manufacturer's authorised representative in the EU for product
safety is Oxford University Press España S.A. of el Parque Empresarial
San Fernando de Henares, Avenida de Castilla, 2 – 28830 Madrid
(www.oup.es/en).

Kerfuffle Bird

Helen Docherty

Gwen Millward

OXFORD
UNIVERSITY PRESS

The Hushlings of Hushville were always polite.

They kept all their feelings shut in, very tight.

They spoke in soft voices; a whisper was best,

and after each meal they would all take a rest.

Every Hushling seemed happy,
except for one:
Maeve.

She knew how a Hushling was meant to behave . . .

But she longed to be noisy, to run and to shout;

she longed to let some of her Big Feelings out.

Maeve's parents, she knew, would be very ashamed.

So, she tried hard to keep all her Big Feelings tamed.

Then, one day Maeve spotted an egg:
huge, and blue.

What was it doing there?
Nobody knew.

The Hushlings agreed, having each had their say,
they should leave it alone, and it might go away.

But the egg didn't go. Three days later, in fact, they saw a big change. Yes, the egg's shell had **cracked!**

The Hushlings all watched.
No one uttered a word . . .

as the egg split apart,

and out stepped a **strange bird.**

He gazed all around.

Then he opened his beak . . .

And let out a glorious, deafening . . .

SSSSHRIIIIIIIIIEK!

The Hushlings, aghast (all but one), quickly scattered.

Their nerves had been **shaken.**

Their peace had been **shattered!**

'What's up with them?' asked the bird, in surprise.

'Well, you see,' Maeve explained, 'we're not used to loud cries.'

'Oh, I'm perfectly harmless.
They should have all stayed!

I'm just a **Kerfuffle Bird**;
that's how I'm made.

So, hey! Where's the party?
Are you coming, too?
I'll give you a ride, so you get
the best view!'

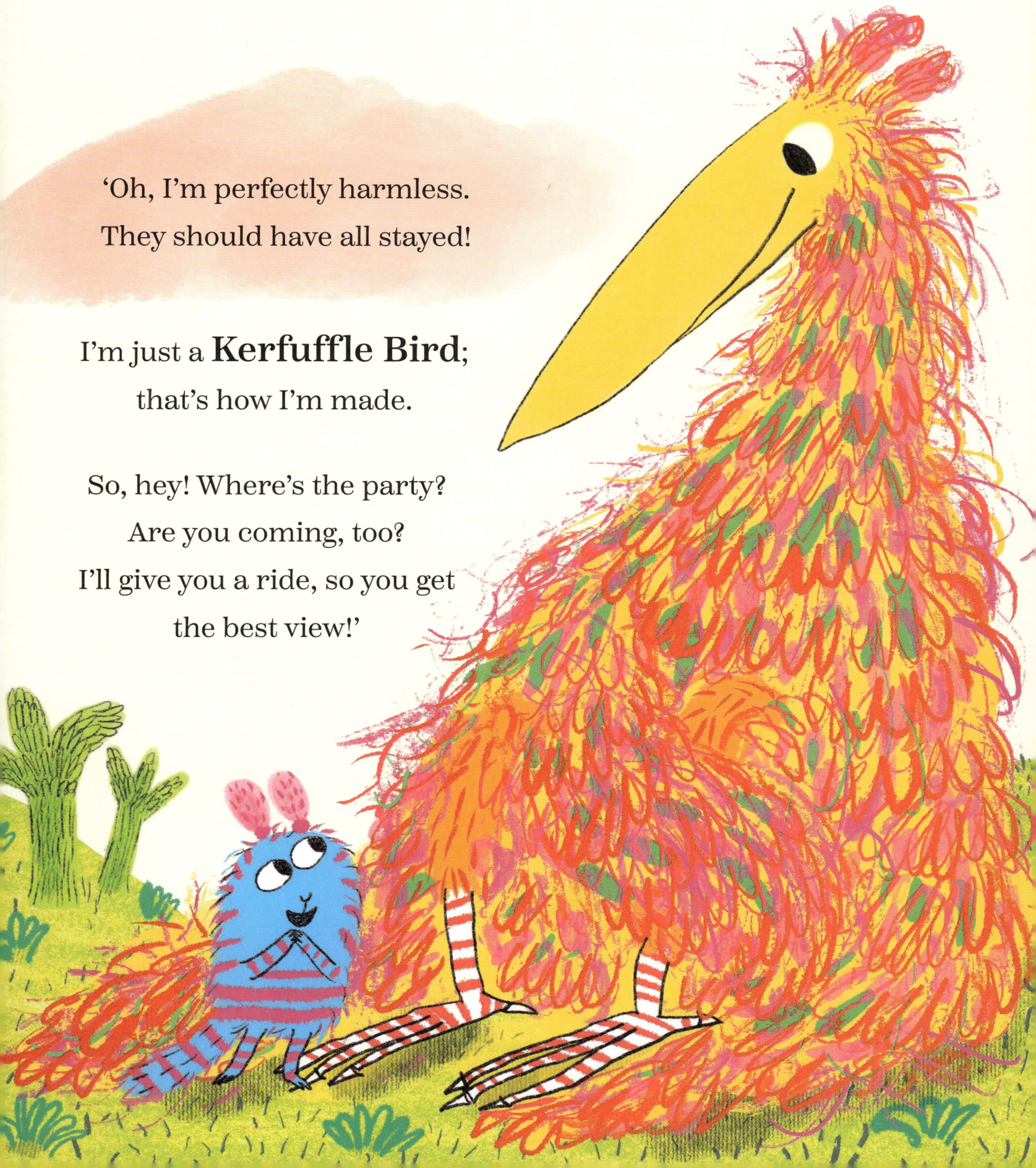

No other Hushling would ever have dared.
But Maeve was quite different; *she* wasn't scared.

'Hold on!' cried Kerfuffle Bird,
looping the loop.

They dived

and they soared,

with a SHRIEK

and a WHOOP!

'And now,' said Kerfuffle Bird,
'Where's the fiesta?'

The Hushlings were having a quiet siesta

when—**suddenly**—something disrupted the calm.
The Hushlings leapt out of their beds in alarm.

A terrible SCREECHING;

a FLAPPING of wings;

a BUMPING and THUMPING

and BASHING of things!

Maeve's parents were startled
to see such a scene.
'We were so worried, Maeve!
Where have you been?'

And they hurried her back to
their house, just before . . .

. . . an unwelcome guest flew
straight in through the door.

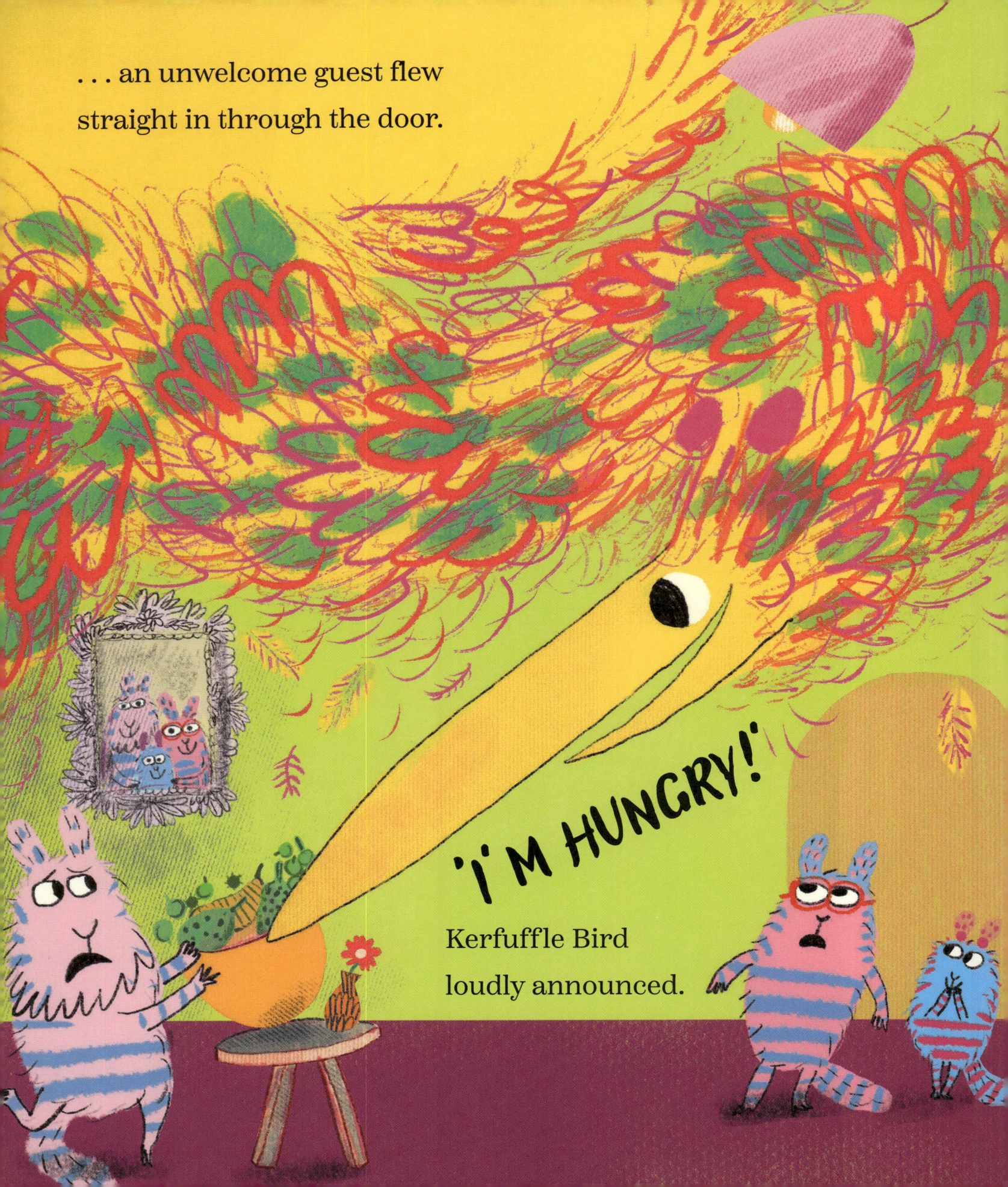

'I'M HUNGRY!'

Kerfuffle Bird
loudly announced.

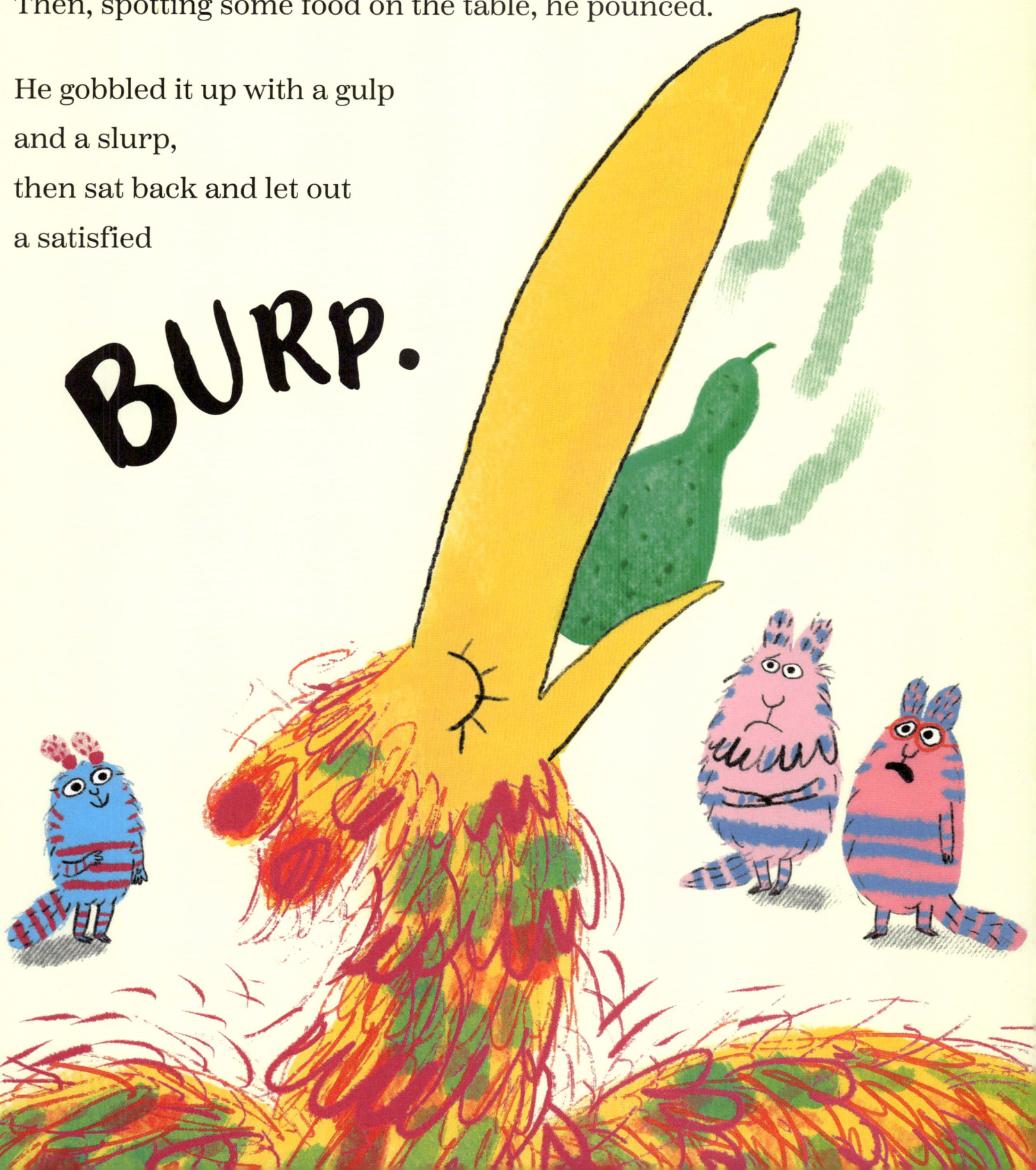

Then, spotting some food on the table, he pounced.

He gobbled it up with a gulp
and a slurp,
then sat back and let out
a satisfied

BURP.

That week, life in Hushville was all a-kerfuffle.
The bird made a racket that no one could muffle.

He SQUAWKED

and he WARBLED

and sang out of tune.

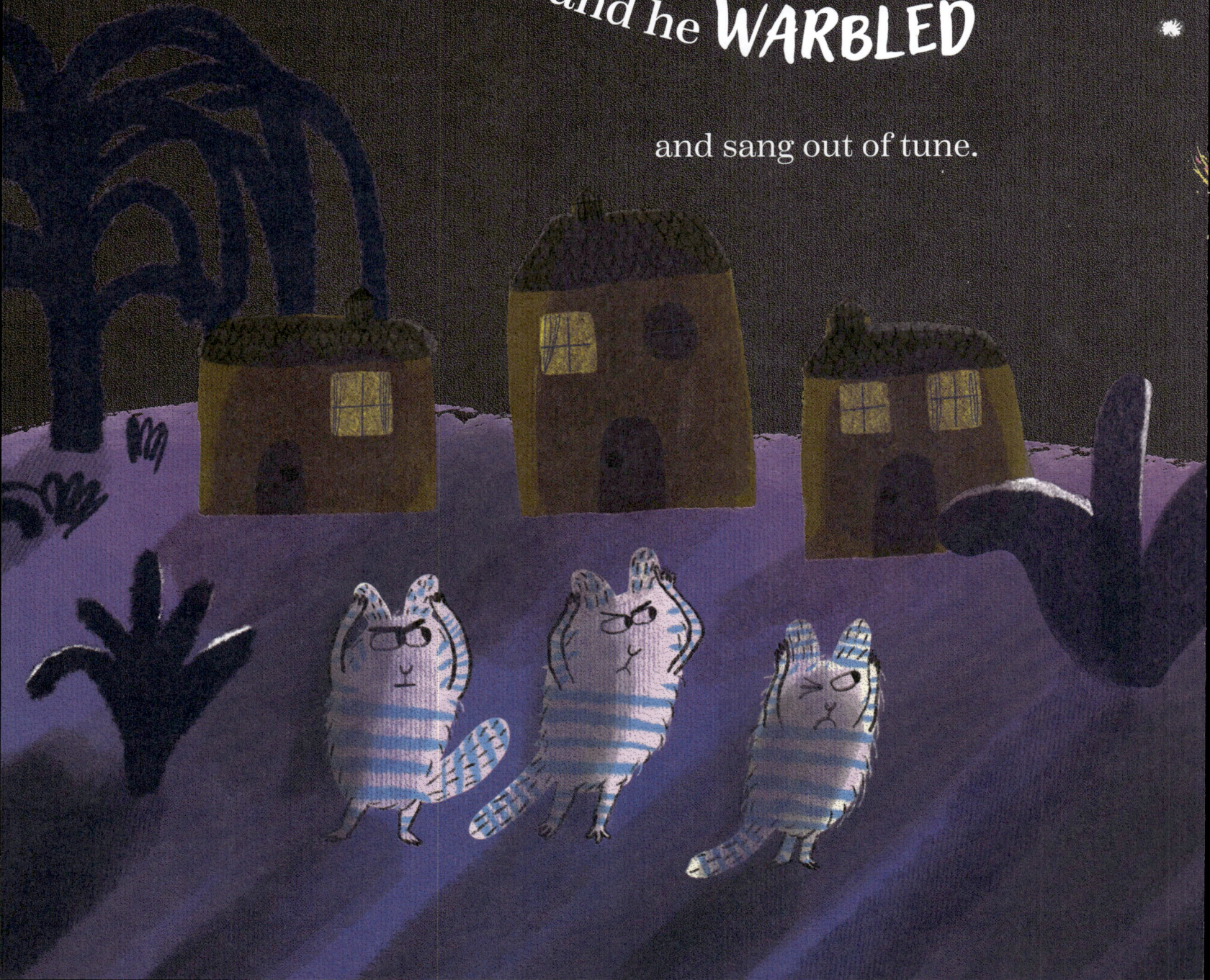

He danced a wild jig by the light of the moon.

He **TANGLED** their washing

and **RUFFLED** their hair.

He **SPAT** all his melon seeds into the air.

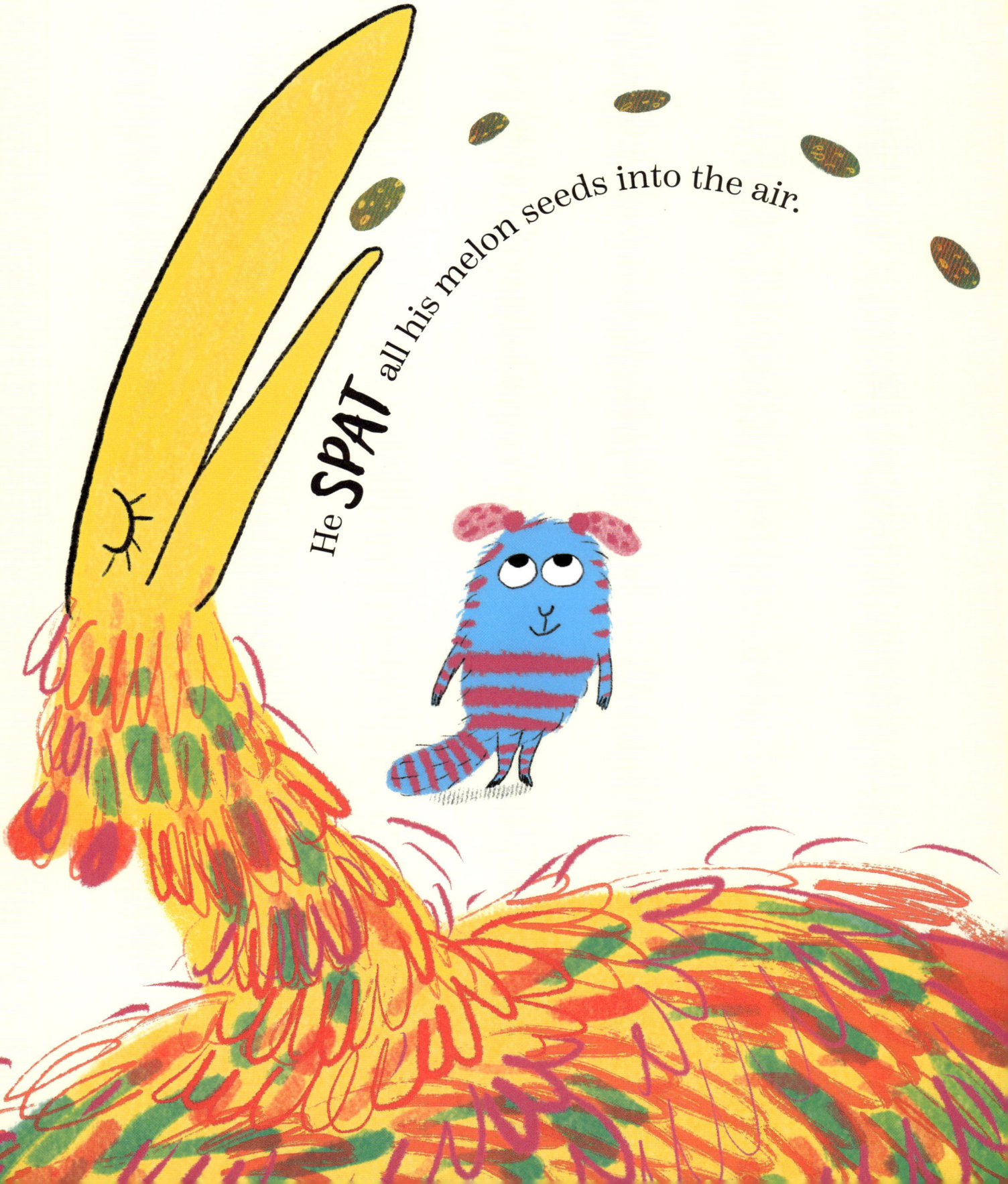

The Hushlings said nothing. They kept it all in.
But their patience was wearing incredibly thin.

ZZZZZZ

Then, one night, at bedtime, he kept them awake
with a **SNORING** so loud, it made every house shake.

And then—something happened that no
one expected.
All those feelings the Hushlings had
quietly collected . . .

ZZZZ

Exploded like **fireworks**

into the sky!

Out of everyone there,
only Maeve could think why.
She knew that if feelings are held in too tight,
they can burst out and give you a terrible fright.

And when it was over, they all stopped and stared.
Even Kerfuffle Bird looked a bit scared.

'I'll leave you in peace, then.'
He hung his head low,

then shuffled
around and got
ready to go.

STOP!

shouted Maeve. She pushed her way through.
'If Kerfuffle Bird leaves, then I'm going to go, too!
It's good to be noisy, to dance and to shout.
It's good to let some of our Big Feelings out!'

Maeve's parents stepped forwards.
'We knew this was brewing.
What happened tonight was
NOT the bird's doing!'

'Perhaps if we'd given our feelings
some air,
We wouldn't have lost it!
We just didn't dare.'

The Hushlings all nodded.
They knew it was true.
'Please stay with us, Maeve—
and Kerfuffle Bird, too!'

From then on, things in Hushville
were never the same.

The Hushlings, you'll find, are a little less tame.

They go to bed later. They've started a choir.
And often, they sit and sing songs round the fire.

Kerfuffle Bird's mellowed. He's calmer these days,
and he tries not to make TOO much noise when he plays.

But one day a week, he and Maeve will go out,
and have a wild time while they're flying about.

And the rest of the Hushlings?
You've probably guessed . . .

They all settle down
to enjoy a good rest.